Ladybird  Readers

MOOMIN

The Birthday Button

Series Editor: Sorrel Pitts
Text adapted by Mary Taylor

LADYBIRD BOOKS

UK | USA | Canada | Ireland | Australia
India | New Zealand | South Africa

Ladybird Books is part of the Penguin Random House group of companies
whose addresses can be found at global.penguinrandomhouse.com.
www.penguin.co.uk   www.puffin.co.uk   www.ladybird.co.uk

Text adapted from 'Moomin and the Birthday Button', first published by Puffin Books Ltd, 2010
This version published by Ladybird Books Ltd, 2019
001

Characters and artwork are the original creation of Tove Jansson
Text and illustrations copyright © Moomin Characters™, 2019
All rights reserved

Printed in China

A CIP catalogue record for this book is available from the British Library

ISBN: 978-0-241-36528-1

All correspondence to:
Ladybird Books
Penguin Random House Children's
80 Strand, London WC2R 0RL

MIX
Paper from
responsible sources
FSC® C018179
www.fsc.org
FSC

Ladybird Readers

MOOMIN

The Birthday Button

Based on the original stories
by Tove Jansson

Picture words

 Moomin

 Moominmamma

 Moominpappa

 Snufkin

 Snorkmaiden

 Sniff

Little My

gold button

pebble

shell

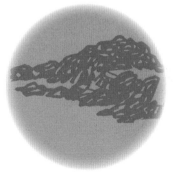

seaweed

treasure chest

Moomin is very happy
this morning.

"It's my birthday!" he says.

"Happy birthday, Moomin!"
say Moominmamma and
Moominpappa.

They give Moomin a
gold button.

"What a beautiful button!"
he says. "Thank you!"

"Hello, Snufkin!" says Moomin. "Look! I have a gold button!"

"Sorry!" says Snufkin.
"I can't talk now."

"Hello, Sniff!" Moomin
says. "Look! I have a
gold button!"

"Sorry!" Sniff says. "I can't
talk now."

Then, Moomin goes to
the beach.

"Snorkmaiden! Little My!
Look!" says Moomin. "I have
a beautiful gold button!"

"Sorry!" they say.
"We can't talk now."

Moomin's friends do not see his new button.

They do not talk to him.

Moomin is very sad.

"It's my birthday, but my friends aren't happy for me," Moomin says.

"Don't worry!" Moominmamma says. "Let's make your birthday cake!"

Moomin loves cake,
but he is very sad.

Then, he hears his friends.

"Moomin! Come here!"
they say.

Sniff has a box in his hands.

"This is for you," say
Moomin's friends.

"The box is from me!"
says Snufkin.

"The shells are from me!"
says Snorkmaiden.

"The pebbles are from me!" says Sniff.

"The seaweed is from me!" says Little My.

"It's a treasure chest for you!" they say.

Then, they eat cake and
sing "Happy Birthday!"

"Thank you!" says Moomin.
He is very happy.

Activities

The key below describes the skills practiced in each activity.

 Spelling and writing

 Reading

 Speaking

 Critical thinking

Preparation for the Cambridge Young Learners exams

1 **Circle the correct picture.** 📖

1 This is Moomin.

2 This is Sniff.

3 This is Moominpappa.

4 This is Snufkin.

2 Match the words to the pictures.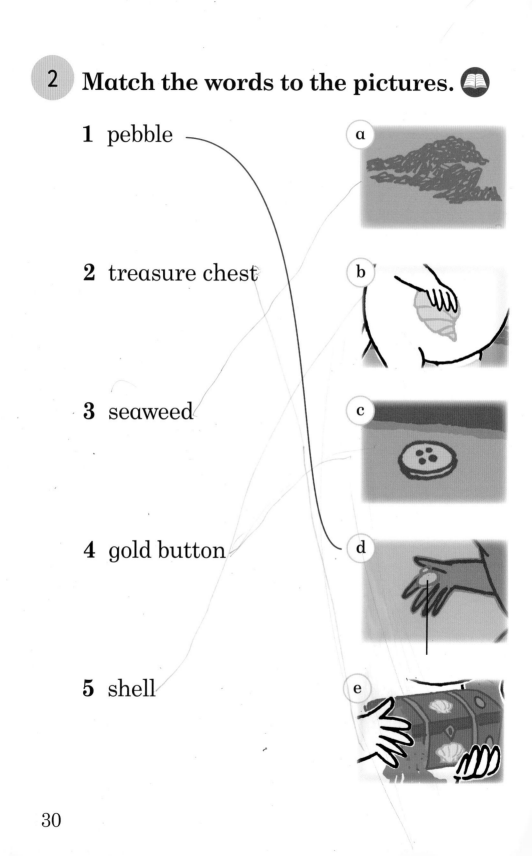

1 pebble

2 treasure chest

3 seaweed

4 gold button

5 shell

a

b

c

d

e

3 **Look at the letters. Write the words.**

1 (r o g m n i n)

It is ...morning....

2 (p h y a p)

Moomin is very ...happy....

3 (d h i a r y b t)

It is Moomin's ...birthday....

4 (d l o g)

Moominmamma and Moominpappa give Moomin a ...gold... button.

5 (u t l e b f a u i)

Moomin says, "What a ...beautiful... button!"

4 **Ask and answer the questions with a friend.** 💬 ❓

"Happy birthday, Moomin!" say Moominmamma and Moominpappa.

They give Moomin a gold button.

"What a beautiful button!" he says. "Thank you!"

1

> Why is Moomin happy today?

> It's his birthday.

2 What color is the button?

3 Where do you wear a button?

4 Does Moomin like the gold button?

5 **Read the text and choose the correct answers.**

1 Moomin says, " . . . birthday!"

  a It's my

  b It's your

2 Moominmamma and Moominpappa . . . "Happy birthday, Moomin!"

  a say

  b says

3 They give Moomin . . . gold button.

  a an

  b a

4 Moomin says, "Thank . . . !"

  a you

  b your

6 **Look at the picture.**
Write *yes* or *no*.

1 Moomin can see Snufkin. _yes_

2 Snufkin has a gold button. No

3 Moomin has a ball. No

4 Snufkin has a green hat. Yes

5 There are some trees and
flowers. Yes

7 **Circle the correct answers.** 📖 🔵

1 Can Snufkin talk to Moomin now?
  a No, he cannot.
  b Yes, he can.

2 What does Moomin say to Sniff?
  a He says, "It's my birthday!"
  b He says, "Look! I have a gold button!"

3 Can Sniff talk to Moomin now?
  a No, he cannot.
  b Yes, he can.

4 Who does Moomin see after Sniff?
  a He sees Snufkin.
  b He sees Snorkmaiden and Little My.

35

8 Find the words.

n h k o b i r t h d a y

m o m l p

h a p p y w k f s d n t a l k

p a o f u h e l l o s p b j i g o l d

n p l k j a d b u t t o n

birthday

happy

talk

hello

gold

button

9 **Circle the correct words.** 📖

1 Snorkmaiden and Little My are
   at the . . .
   a park.
   b beach.

2 Moomin says, "Look! I have a . . .
   gold button!"
   a big
   b beautiful

3 Snorkmaiden and Little My say, . . .
   a "Sorry. We can't talk now."
   b "Hello. We can talk now."

4 Moomin is very . . .
   a sad.
   b happy.

10 **Circle the correct sentences.**

1
    a Little My can talk to Moomin.
    b Little My cannot talk to Moomin.

2
    a Moomin's friends see his button.
    b Moomin's friends do not see his button.

3
    a Moomin's friends do not talk to him.
    b Moomin's friends talk to him.

4
    a Moomin is very sad.
    b Moomin is very happy.

11 **Find the words.**

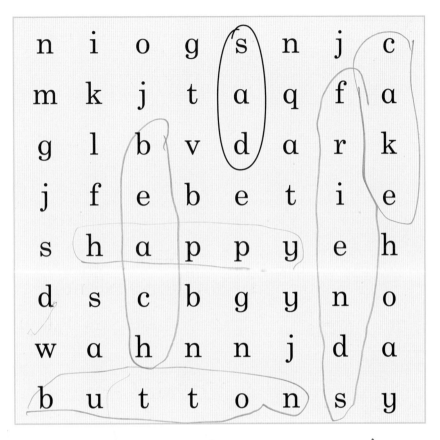

n	i	o	g	s	n	j	c
m	k	j	t	a	q	f	a
g	l	b	v	d	a	r	k
j	f	e	b	e	t	i	e
s	h	a	p	p	y	e	h
d	s	c	b	g	y	n	o
w	a	h	n	n	j	d	a
b	u	t	t	o	n	s	y

sad

happy

friends

button

cake

beach

39

12 **Look at the picture and read the questions. Write the answers.**

"It's my birthday, but my friends aren't happy for me," Moomin says.

"Don't worry!" Moominmamma says. "Let's make your birthday cake!"

1 Who is Moomin talking to?

He is talking to Moominmamma.

2 Why is Moomin sad?

His friends are not *a carling* for him.

3 What does Moominmamma say?

She says, "Let's make your *birthday* cake!"

13 Circle the correct words.

1 Moomin loves

  a cake.   **b** apples.

2 Moomin is very

  a hot.   **b** sad.

3 Then, Moomin hears

  a Moominmamma.

  b his friends.

4 Moomin's friends say,

  "Moomin! Come

  a here!"   **b** there!"

14 **Look and read. Choose the correct words, and write them on the lines.**

Sniff has a box in his hands.

"This is for you," say Moomin's friends.

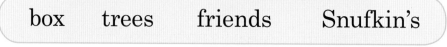

box   trees   friends   Snufkin's

1 Sniff has a .... box .... in his hands.

2 Moomin's .... friends .... say, "This is for you."

3 Little My is on .... Snufkin's .... head.

4 There are some .... trees .... behind Moomin's friends.

15 Who says this?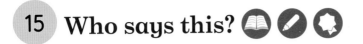

Snorkmaiden   Sniff   Little My   Snufkin

1 "The box is from me!"

says ___Snufkin___.

2 "The shells are from me!"

says ___Snorkmaiden___.

3 "The pebbles are from me!"

says ___Sniff___.

4 "The seaweed is from me!"

says ___Little my___.

16 Talk about the two pictures with a friend. How are they different? Use the words in the box. ◯

happy sad gold button flowers Moominmamma box friends cake

In picture a, Moomin is sad.

In picture b, Moomin is happy.

17 Do the crossword. 📖 ✏️

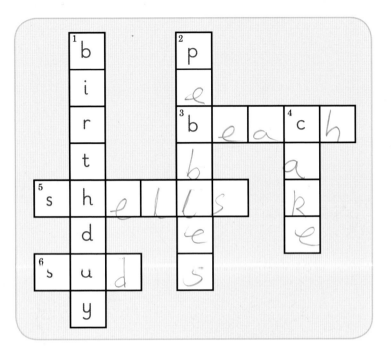

Across

3 Moomin sees Snorkmaiden and Little My at the . . .

5 Snorkmaiden gives Moomin the . . .

6 Moomin's friends cannot talk to him, and he is . . .

Down

1 Today is Moomin's . . .

2 Sniff gives Moomin the . . .

4 Moominmamma makes a . . . for Moomin.

45

18 Look and read. Put a ✓ or a ✗ in the boxes.

1 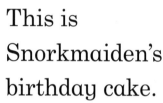 Snufkin gives Moomin a gold button. **✗**

2 This is Snorkmaiden's birthday cake. **✗**

3 Moomin's friends give him a treasure chest. ✓

4  Moomin and his friends eat cake and sing. ✓

19 Put a by all the things in this book.

1 a gold button	✓	**8** a banana	☐
2 a cat	☐	**9** a cake	✓
3 shells	✓	**10** friends	✓
4 a park	☐	**11** birds	☐
5 a beach	✓	**12** trees	✓
6 a treasure chest	✓	**13** a bus	☐
7 pebbles	✓	**14** flowers	✓

Ladybird Readers	Ladybird Readers	Ladybird Readers	Ladybird Readers	Ladybird Readers
Level 1	Level 1	Level 1	Level 1	Level 1
Anansi Helps a Friend	Cinderella	The Enormous Turnip	Jon's Football Team	The Magic Porridge Pot
978–0–241–25409–7	978–0–241–25407–3	978–0–241–25408–0	978–0–241–25411–0	978–0–241–25406–6
Level 1	Level 1	Level 1	Level 1	Level 1
Rex the Big Dinosaur	Fairy Friends	Topsy and Tim Go to the Zoo	Topsy and Tim Go to the Farm	Topsy and Tim Go to London
978–0–241–29741–4	978–0–241–28351–6	978–0–241–25414–1	978–0–241–28355–4	978-0-241-29743-8
Level 1	Level 1	Level 1	Level 1	Level 1
On the Farm	Cars	Peter Rabbit Goes to the Island	Peter Rabbit and the Radish Robber	The Tale of Peter Rabbit
978–0–241–25413–4	978–0–241–28354–7	978–0–241–25415–8	978-0-241-29742-1	978-0-241-31614-6
Level 1	Level 1	Level 1	Level 1	Level 1
In the Garden	Fun with Old Things	The Fair	Daddy Pig's Old Chair	On a Boat
978–0–241–26220–7	978–0–241–26219–1	978–0–241–28357–8	978–0–241–28356–1	978-0-241-29744-5
Level 1	Level 1	Level 1	Level 1	Level 1
Going Swimming	Going to the Moon	Pom Pom is Grumpy	The Birthday Button	Decepticons in the Scrapyard
978–0–241–31613–9	978–0–241–36544–1	978–0–241–35794–1	978-0-241-36528-1	978-0-241-31943-7
Level 1	Level 1	Level 1		
Baby Animals	Deserts	Animal Colors		
978-0-241-29745-2	978-0-241-31608-5	978-0-241-35792-7		

Now you're ready for Level 2!